This Orchard book

belongs to

....

For Catie – our very own superhero!
M.B.

For Erin and Isla
S.R.

ORCHARD BOOKS

First published in Great Britain in 2017 by The Watts Publishing Group

9 10 8

Text © Mike Brownlow, 2017
Illustrations © Simon Rickerty, 2017

The moral rights of the author and illustrator have been asserted.

ISBN 978 1 40834 627 3

Printed and bound in China

MIX
Paper from
responsible sources
FSC
www.fsc.org
FSC® C104740

Orchard Books
An imprint of Hachette Children's Group
Part of The Watts Publishing Group Limited
Carmelite House, 50 Victoria Embankment, London EC4Y 0DZ

An Hachette UK Company
www.hachette.co.uk

www.hachettechildrens.co.uk

TEN LITTLE SUPERHEROES

Mike Brownlow  Simon Rickerty

ORCHARD

Ten Little Super-Kids, flying through the air,
Spot the League of Bad Guys plotting in their lair.

"We have to save the city
and we have to act right now!"

Ten Little Super-Kids all say,

"POW!"

Monstro shouts, "You Kids can't stop me! Victory will be mine!"

BISH! BASH! BOSH!

goes Hippo Man.

Now there are . . .

...S

Metro Hall is battered by the

Bad Guys' shocking tricks.

7

Swish!
go the Kraken's arms!

Now there are . . .

...five.

5

Things are tense.
The Bad Guys try to
batter down the door!

SNIP!

SNIP!

SNIP!

go Crab Man's claws.

Now there are . . .

...four.

"After them!" the villains cry.
The Kids are forced
to flee.

4

Jab!

go the Hedgehog's darts.

Now there are . . .

...three.

The Super-Kids are hiding,
while they puzzle what to do.

"HEAR

... two.

Monstro tries a wicked ploy –
using sound to stun.

BOOOOOO

2

OOM!!

goes his Sonic Beam.

Now there's only . . .

. . . one.

Monstro's gang is jubilant. They think they've won the day.

But while he hides, the last Kid calls his battered friends to say . . .

"I'll throw our Super Smoke Bomb to delay them if I can.

Quick! Get back to Metro Hall. I have a cunning plan!"

They fly round at super speed to send the Bad Guys spinning.
Monstro's Gang turn dizzy and HOORAY! the Kids are winning!
Then with a . . .

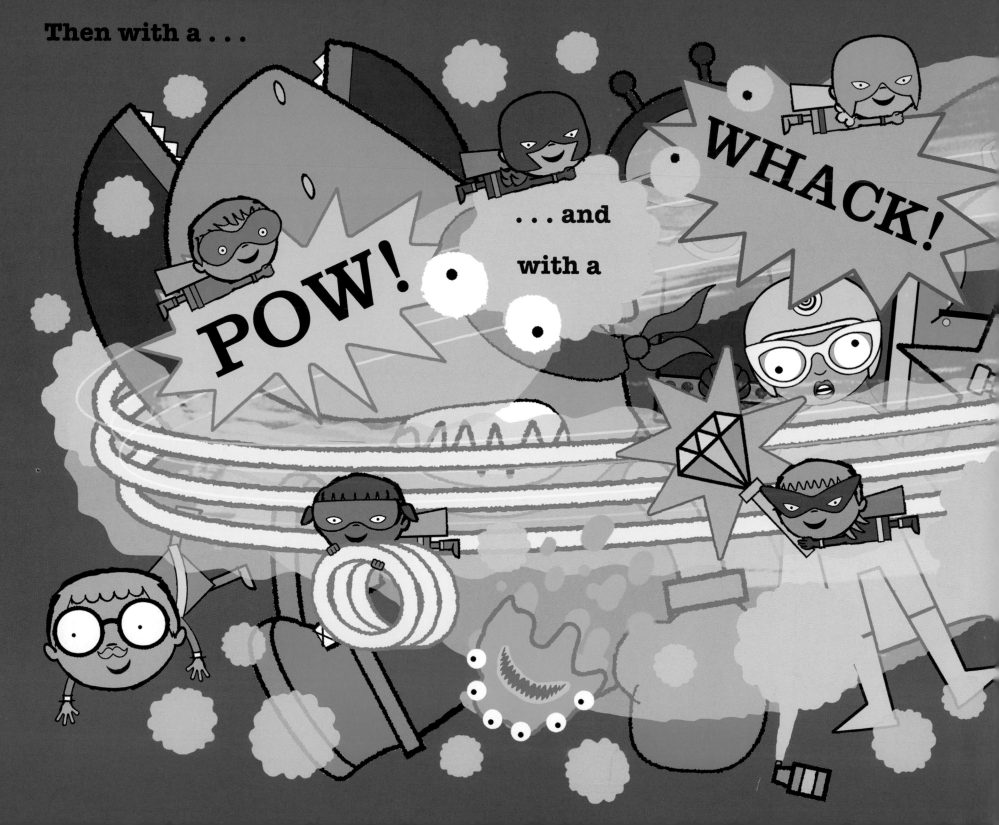

Befuddled by the super speed, the Bad Guys give up hope.

It's off to jail for Monstro's Gang, tied up with Super-Rope.

"We hate you pesky Super-Kids!

Without you we'd have won!

wails Monstro, looking glum.

Ten Little Super-Kids all say,

"POW!"